DO NOT BRING YOUR DRAGON TO RECESS

WRITTEN BY JULIE GASSMAN
ILLUSTRATED BY ANDY ELKERTON

Capstone Young Readers
a capstone imprint

All morning your've worked and given your best.
You wrote, you read, you took a math test.

It's now time for recess, your well-earned break.
But before you head out, **please** avoid this mistake . . .

The rules of the playground are hard for a beast.
He'll break the first one as soon as released.

He'll run down the halls, **shout** to his friends.
He'll **bump** into the principal with his pokey rear end!

Out on the monkey bars things won't improve.
Your dramatic dragon will ruin your **groove**.

She cries and she cries. Her arms are too small.
If she hangs from her tail, the whole line will stall.

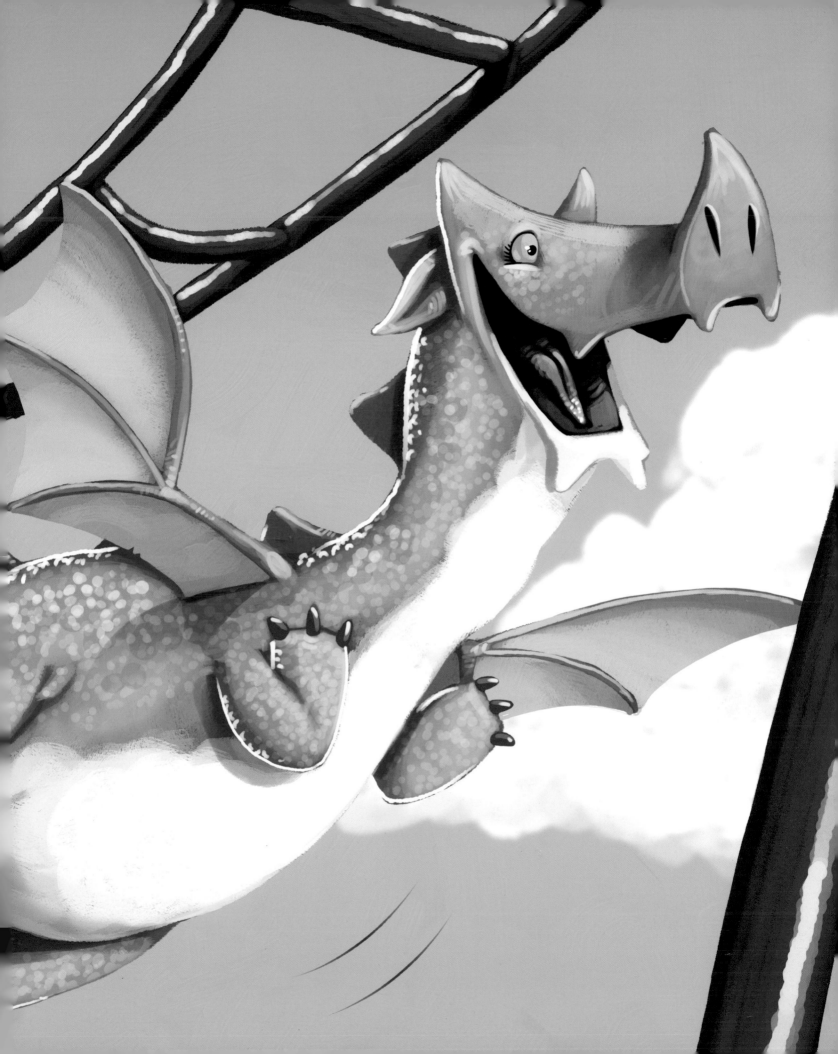

Maybe he'll vow to keep his feet on the ground
and volunteer to push the merry-go-round.

He'll start out slow, but soon he will run.
Then the ride becomes more scary than fun.

I see what you're saying, and I admit to you
that a dragon at recess could create a real zoo.

But my dragon is smart. He can learn all the rules.
He'll listen to teachers when he's playing at school.

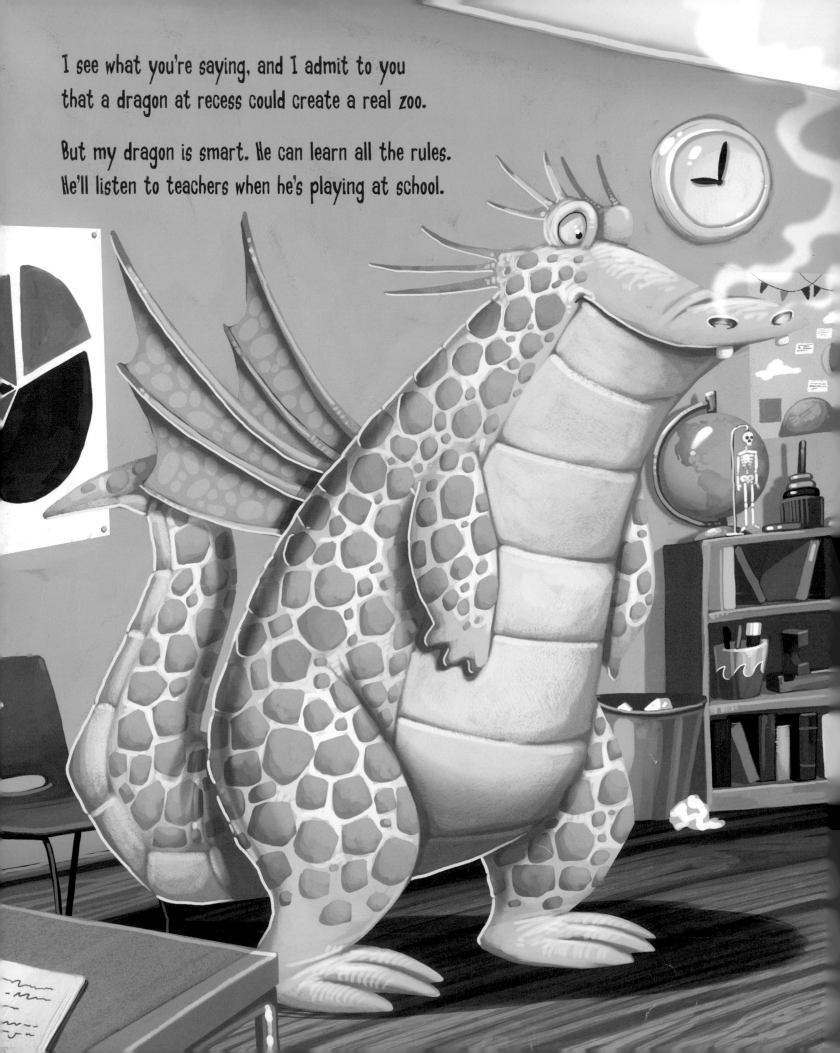

He'll be **patient** and **take turns**.

He'll **share** all the toys.

He'll be **respectful** and **kind** to all girls and boys.

I know he can do it! You just have to say **yes**!
May I **please** bring my dragon to play at recess?

In my mind, dragons are all fire and wings.
I didn't know they were interested in slides and swings.

But I believe everyone deserves his or her chance
to run and to climb, to chase and to dance.

So if your dragon's respectful, well, then, I guess . . .

HE'S MORE THAN WELCOME AT OUR SCHOOL RECESS!

ABOUT THE AUTHOR

The youngest in a family of nine children, Julie Gassman grew up in Howard, South Dakota. After college, she traded in small-town life for the world of magazine publishing in New York City. She now lives in southern Minnesota with her husband and their three children. Julie's favorite recess activity was playing tether ball, a game that would be quite challenging for a dragon with short arms.

ABOUT THE ILLUSTRATOR

After fourteen years as a graphic designer, Andy decided to go back to his illustrative roots as a children's book illustrator. Since 2002 he has produced work for picture books, educational books, advertising, and toy design. Andy has worked for clients all over the world. He currently lives in a small tourist town on the west coast of Scotland with his wife and three children.

Do NOT Take Your Dragon to Recess is published by
Capstone Young Readers, a Capstone imprint
1710 Roe Crest Drive, North Mankato, Minnesota 56003
www.mycapstone.com

Copyright © 2018 Capstone Young Readers

Library of Congress Cataloging-in-Publication Data
Names: Gassman, Julie, author. | Elkerton, Andy, illustrator.
Title: Do not bring your dragon to recess / by Julie Gassman; illustrated by Andy Elkerton.

Description: North Mankato, Minnesota : Picture Window Books, [2018]
Series: Fiction picture books | Summary: Told in rhyme, a child is cautioned about the problems his dragon is likely to cause at school recess, even if it does not mean to.

Identifiers: LCCN 2018009427 (print) | LCCN 2018009719 (ebook)
ISBN 9781515828440 (eBook PDF) | ISBN 9781515828433 (library binding)
ISBN 9781684360352 (paper over board)

Subjects: LCSH: Dragons—Juvenile fiction. School recess breaks—Juvenile fiction. Schools—Juvenile fiction. | Stories in rhyme. CYAC: Stories in rhyme. | Dragons—Fiction. Recess—Fiction. Schools—Fiction. | LCGFT: Stories in rhyme

Classification: LCC PZ7.G2147 (ebook) | LCC PZ8.3.G199 Dl 2018 (print)
DDC [E]—dc23 LC record available at https://lccn.loc.gov/2018009427

Designer: Ashlee Suker

Printed and bound in the United States of America.
PA017